GREETINGS FROM

Vera B. Williams
STORY AND PICTURES

and *Jennifer Williams*
MORE PICTURES

STRINGBEAN'S TRIP TO THE SHINING SEA

SCHOLASTIC INC.

New York Toronto London Auckland Sydney

ISBN 0-590-44851-X
Copyright © 1988 by Vera B. Williams and Jennifer Williams. All rights reserved. Published by Scholastic Inc., 730 Broadway, New York, NY 10003, by arrangement with Greenwillow Books, a division of William Morrow & Company, Inc. BLUE RIBBON is a registered trademark of Scholastic Inc.
12 11 10 9 8   9/7
                                                    08
Printed in the U.S.A.
First Scholastic printing, October 1989

POST CARD

Dear Readers,

Here are the postcards and snap-shots that Stringbean Coe and his brother Fred sent home to their mother, their father, and their grandfather. They're from the long trip Stringbean made one summer with Fred in Fred's truck with the little house built on the back.

Their grandfather made this album for the family.

Love
Vera, Jenny, and the people at Greenwillow Books

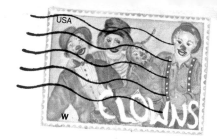

THIS SPACE FOR ADDRESS

Readers

Planet Earth

The Solar System

The Universe

ARTIST: VERA B. WILLIAMS

NAMES & PLACES

❧ POSTCARD ❧

Dear Ma, Pa, Grandpa and Potato,

We didn't even get started right after we said goodbye to you. We stopped to buy me a hat like Fred's. Then we had to stop at Moe's junkyard for an extra spare tire.

I hope the photos you took with Grandpa's old camera turn out. You'll see the truck looks really great - not like a piece of junk like you said.

You know what Mr Moe even said to Freddy? "I'll buy that truck back from you for a good price." My brother is not nuts. He told Mr. Moe no way and that this was an important trip we had to take.

Mr Moe gave me a pretty postcard he had saved from a long time x ago. I'll send it too.

love Stringbean

GRANDPA, I PROMISE TO TAKE PERFECT CARE OF YOUR CAMERA.

ARTIST: VERA B. WILLIAMS

PUT YOUR BUSINESS ON A CARD

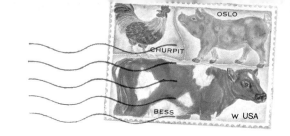

COE FAMILY

THIS SPACE FOR ADDRESS

COE SPRINGS MOTEL

JELOWAY, Ks.

66708

P.S. Grandpa tell Potato I miss her a lot. But don't let her bark loud at Fred's rabbit like she does when she gets mad at us.   S.

FRED

STRINGBEAN'S SCHOOL PHOTO

FRED'S AUTO REPAIR

If Fred can't fix it maybe it can't be fixed. -Fred

THE MORNING BEFORE THEY LEFT [OUTSIDE FRED'S GARAGE]

THE TRUCK WITH THE HOUSE FRED AND STRINGBEAN BUILT ON THE BACK. STRINGBEAN IS HOLDING THE PIE WE BAKED THEM FOR A SEND-OFF. HE CLIMBED UP AND PICKED ALL THE CHERRIES OFF OUR TREE THE DAY BEFORE THEY LEFT.

POTATO JUST AFTER STRINGBEAN LEFT. SHE WOULDN'T GET UP OR EAT OR DO ANYTHING.

Greetings from the Pacific Ocean

POST CARD

MESSAGE HERE

Dear Ma, Pa and Grandpa

Mr. Moe saved this card from a trip he took a long time ago.

He liked the idea we were going all the way to the Pacific ocean. I showed him, in the map in the road atlas you gave us.

"That's the ticket" he said to me. "The Pacific ocean.. yes. You'll be driving along one day and you'll come through some hills and redwood trees and there she'll be.....THE PACIFIC OCEAN, one of the shining seas, the biggest one too."

He told me to say hello to the seals on the beach for old Mr. Moe. I promised I would.

love
Stringbean

my signature is → → →Stringbean
getting good like yours Grandpa

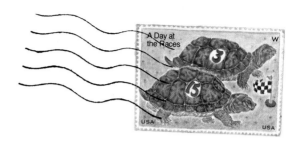

ARTIST: JENNIFER WILLIAMS

SEVEN SEAS CARD CO.

THIS SPACE FOR ADDRESS

Coe Family
Coe Springs Motel
Jeloway, Ks.
66708

Dear Folks,
Please give Lily carrots with her rabbit food. And don't worry about us. Stringbean still doesn't eat much but we're having a great time already.

love
Fred

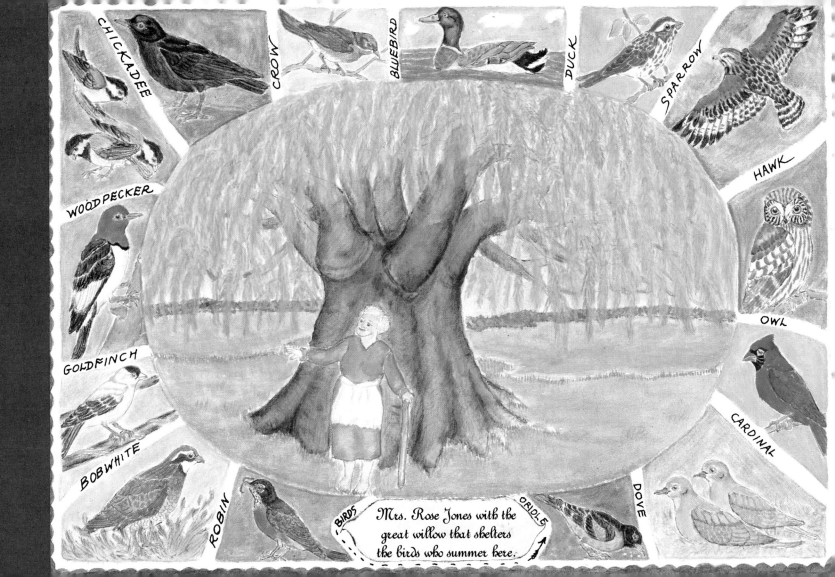

CHICKADEE

CROW

BLUEBIRD

DUCK

SPARROW

HAWK

WOODPECKER

OWL

GOLDFINCH

CARDINAL

BOBWHITE

ROBIN

BIRDS

ORIOLE

DOVE

Mrs. Rose Jones with the great willow that shelters the birds who summer here.

·POST CARD·

Dear Ma, Pa and Grandpa,

  We are sending photos to prove Potato is O.K. and just fine after looking for us the whole night.

  Freddy says he was so excited when he phoned you he's not sure he told you just where she found us. Well it was here. Isn't she smart?

  We were swimming in this lake by a big old willow tree. You know how Potato doesn't like water but she came right on in and landed right on top of me with a big SPLASH. The birds in the willow all flew out. I <u>KNEW</u> she wouldn't stay home without me.
        love from Stringbean and Potato X ×××× ↑ a big dog kiss

ARTIST: JENNIFER WILLIAMS

NATURE CARDS   SERIES #2 — BIRDS

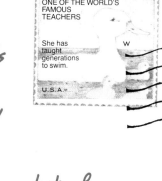

Dear Folks,
Stringbean is <u>utterly</u> and <u>completely</u> and <u>totally</u> happy now. He made a list of special places we should see while I made a sketch for you.

ADDRESS

MR. and MS. COE and MR. F.M.
COE SPRINGS MOTEL
JELDWAY, KS.
66708

P.S. I am going to get Potato a hat like mine and Fred's.

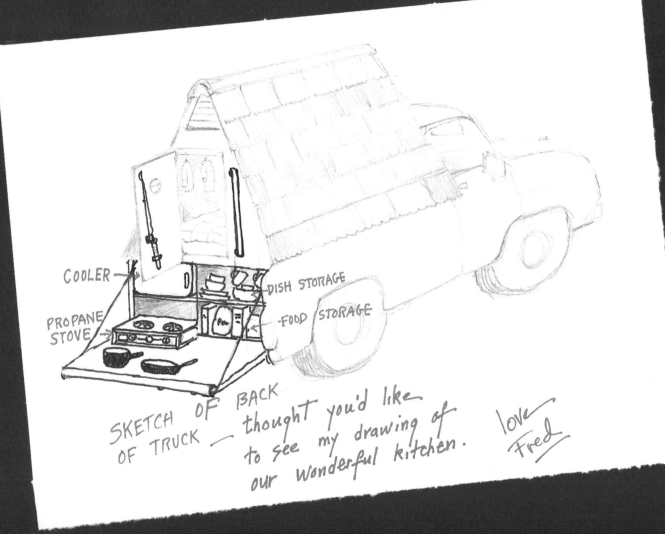

COOLER

DISH STORAGE

PROPANE
STOVE

FOOD STORAGE

SKETCH OF BACK
OF TRUCK — thought you'd like
to see my drawing of
our wonderful kitchen.

love
Fred

This sod house was built in 1871 by Mrs. Lovey Johnson. The first midwife to practice her profession in this area, summer and winter she rode her pinto over the prairie to help at births. She lived on this spot till she was one hundred years old. Many a child was named for Lovey Johnson by grateful parents.

LOVEY ANDREWS

LOVEY TUCKER

MRS. LOVEY JOHNSON, MIDWIFE

JOHNSON PETERSON

Post Card

Dear Ma, Pa and Grandpa,

   We stopped to see what this place was. It's very old. It's a history place. We watched the shadows of the clouds go over.

   I think the clouds here are the ghosts [good ghosts] of those people the midwife helped to get born. I think they are looking after her little empty old house.

                    love from me (Stringbean)

Dear Folks,
   This was the first time Stringbean stopped talking since we left Jeloway! I guess you did warn me.
   Driving away from this special old place it got so dark and poured so much we had to stop. Water to the hubcaps! We curled up in our house in the back and ate peanuts and listened to the radio.
                              love Fred

P.S. We are thinking up a name for the truck.
Do you like
HARRY-THE-CHARIOT
or WINNIE-THE-WHEEL?

★ CREATED BY VERA B. WILLIAMS ★

★ LUCKY HISTORY CARDS ★

S---n-b--n

ADDRESS

The COE FAMILY
COE SPRINGS
MOTEL
JELOWAY, KS.
66708

PPS. DO YOU LIKE MY LETTERING?
Maybe I will be a sign painter someday.

W U.S.A.
S.A.M.
MADE IN USA

LAZY RIVER CAMPGROUND

EASILY REACHED FROM MANY ROADS, WE HAVE PLENTY OF WATER, HAY, AND SHADE TREES. THIS IS A FAVORITE STOPPING PLACE FOR TRAVELING CIRCUSES. EARLY-RISING CAMPERS ARE OFTEN REWARDED BY THE SIGHT OF A CIRCUS ON ITS WAY AT DAWN.

Dear Ma, Pa and Grandpa,
We stayed in the exact same campground as the circus!!☆✳✳⸰
We got here in the dark. Potato and me were asleep already. But in the morning I was looking out at a big old elephant. [really]. But we only got to see them packing up and moving out with their trucks and all their stuff. It was so early there were still stars up in the sky.
After when I was looking around I found one of the clowns great big shoes! I hope they have extras. Freddy says we'll catch up to them so we can give it back. It's a big

funny shoe. I think it's a lucky shoe. Potato loves this shoe!
love Stringbean

ARTIST: JENNIFER WILLIAMS

PUT YOUR BUSINESS ON A CARD

INTERNATIONAL SOMERSAULT GAMES U.S.A.

W

□ □ □ □ THIS SPACE FOR ADDRESS □ □ □ □

COE FAMILY

COE SPRINGS MOTEL

JELOWAY, KS.

66708

P.S. We are going to stay at a Buffalo Ranch ~~tomorrow~~ tonight. I am excited. This isn't such good printing because I did it too fast.

Dear Ma,

Remember I cried that time you told me too much hunting had killed off almost every buffalo. NOW THERE ARE BUFFALO AGAIN.

One reason is Mr. Harlee Hawkins. He started this ranch with just 4 wild buffalo. Now there are 200. He is a Sioux. His grandma told him how once buffalo used to cross the river for 6 days and 6 nights. And there were so many passenger pigeons it made the sky dark. There were so many eagles. There were so many elk.

Mr. Hawkins says the exact same thing grandpa says, "Well kid that was then. This is now."

I love the way buffalos have curls growing down their noses. Ask aunt Tina for me, "Would you like if a buffalo came to your beauty parlor for a shampoo?"

Love and hugs x x x x x x

ARTIST: JENNIFER WILLIAMS

NATURE CARDS SERIES #1—ANIMALS

Dear Folks,
I hope Lily is doing well. I'm wishing for a big litter.

Love Fred

FAVORITE SHOES
W   U.S.A

THE COE
FAMILY
COE SPRINGS MOTEL

JELOWAY, KS.

66708

P.S.
So far no trouble with truck. Stringbean checks the oil and tires so don't worry.
x x Stringbean
F.

ANSWER ▷ FOOTHILLS

TAKE A BREATH BEFORE YOU START CLIMBING.
CAMP AT **FOOTHILLS REST.**
FOLLOW THE GREEN ARROWS FROM THE HIGHWAY.

Dear Ma, Pa, Grandpa,
See that place marked with an X ?
That's where we're going to stay tonight.
It's a foothill. They just stick up all of a
sudden like Potato under the covers.
These are the first mountains I was ever
in (on? in?).

Fred says we'll come to mountains
where the snow never melts. We'll be able
to see all over. (maybe we'll get to even see
where those circus trucks went to.) We are
going to stop and see the town where
Grandpa used to be a silver miner.
~~and~~ We're going to climb up and see
the oldest trees in the world. Then
we have to cross the desert.

P.S. Potato likes to bark to the coyotes in
the dark. I'm learning names of stars.
We roasted corn in our fire. It's very good that way.

VERA B. WILLIAMS

THE ODDBALL CARD CO.

USA W — Mary Marshall Brownie Founder, United Dogs of Canada & the U.S.

THIS SPACE FOR ADDRESS

COE FAMILY

COE SPRINGS MOTEL

JELOWAY, KS

66708

xlove, Stringbean x

Did You know there is a star named
BETELGEUSE?

This is how Goldilocks and the three bears might look today.

POST CARD

Bears are not pets. Do not feed them or approach the cubs. Place all food out of bears' reach.

WHAT DID THE BEAR SEE WHEN SHE WENT OVER THE MOUNTAIN?

more and more and more mountains. We saw bears swimming! Really we did.

These mountains are really high. I looked way way down. I saw a car upside down in a creek. Freddy drove so slow around and around the curves. I beeped the horn.

Today we hiked to the top. So far this is the best place. Eagles live up here. I'm going to be a mt. climber. So is Potato.   Love Stringbean

Dear Folks,
Those bears were close! Stringbean fell over holding on to Potato so she wouldn't

go after them. We stood back and made a lot of noise. We sure weren't easy till they swam away.
Love Fred

 HOT-AIR BALLOON
W   INVENTED 1783
USA   USA

THIS SPACE FOR ADDRESS

COE FAMILY

COE SPRINGS MOTEL

JELOWAY, KS.

66708

how is LILY ?

P.S. I hope I will see a Rocky Mt. Bighorn Sheep.

NATURE CARDS — SERIES #1 — ANIMALS — ARTIST: JENNIFER WILLIAMS

JOSEFINA VALDEZ MULLER

Boarding house prop. Fed entire town during great blizzard

FREDERICK MULLER

Miner Organized union of silver miners

ANDREW McKAY

Mine carpenter Built mine support system following great cave-in

DR. EMILY CASTLETON

Physician Founded town's first hospital

MISS ROSE BROWN

Publisher and printer of town's first weekly, *The Silver Dollar Gazette*

MRS. LETTY SOREN AND DAUGHTER MAY

Started first general store on Main Street

NAMES UNKNOWN

Children employed at mine shed

ELY FLASHTAIL

Muleteer and hero of the big cave-in

RON BABCOCK

Millwright and inventor

JOHN TENG

Miner

BONITA LIVESY

Dairy woman and farmer

Visit this graveyard of white stones. It honors miners and their families who trekked here from far places to build a once-famous and busy town in these mountains.

Post Card

Grandpa, your old house is a museum now and they have cards with pictures of your parents on them!

Dear Grandpa (I'm going to try cursive)
We came out of the long long tunnel and it was just like you said. We saw the big old rock crusher on the hill and the broken down houses.

We went everywhere you told us about. They even let you go down in the old mine. We rode on the train that used to take out the silver rocks. I rode with the driver. The shed where you worked when you were a kid is still there. It has a big hole in the roof.

We picked lots of little flowers to put on the graves for great grandmother Josefina and great grandfather Frederick.
love from your Grandson,

Stringbean Cesar Joseph Coe)

P.S. I owe you that quarter Grandpa. The 3 Giants Mts. really do turn purple at sunset.

USA
W
FAVORITE TOOLS

THIS SPACE FOR ADDRESS

MR. FREDERICK MULLER

c/o COE SPRINGS MOTEL

JELOWAY, KS. 66708

P.P.S. Grandpa,
How come you never said all those stories you told us were real History. WOW! K.

The town is now a ghost town, but the canyon is well worth a visit. In late spring over one hundred waterfalls have been counted.

POST CARD

━━━ THIS SPACE FOR MESSAGE ━━━

Dear Ma, Do you believe in GHOSTS?

A man where we stopped to look at rock specimens told us about this canyon. He gave me this card and said we should watch for the ghost horse.

Freddy didn't even want to come here. We had a big *argument. Then he was glad we came. But only because of the waterfalls. We got so hot and our mouths got full of dust driving down the mountains.

Fred says there is no such thing as a ghost but in the night I saw something cloudy moving along the rocks. And I did hear hoof beats.
* Fred and me have some, BIG fights. He only likes history places and fishing and cars. Potato

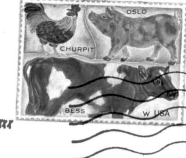

likes the same things I like. Potato and me miss you.
love and kisses xxxx
Stringbean

DESIGNED AND PAINTED FOR FRIENDS OF GHOST TOWNS BY JENNIFER WILLIAMS

━━━ THIS SPACE FOR ADDRESS ━━━

Ms ELENA COE
my mother →
COE SPRINGS MOTEL
JELOWAY, KS. 66708

Dear Folks,
That son of yours, Stringbean sure is stubborn. I guess he takes after Grandpa...... AND
HAPPY BIRTHDAY TO YOU GRANDPA ON YOUR 82nd, I'll call you —
Lots of Love Fred

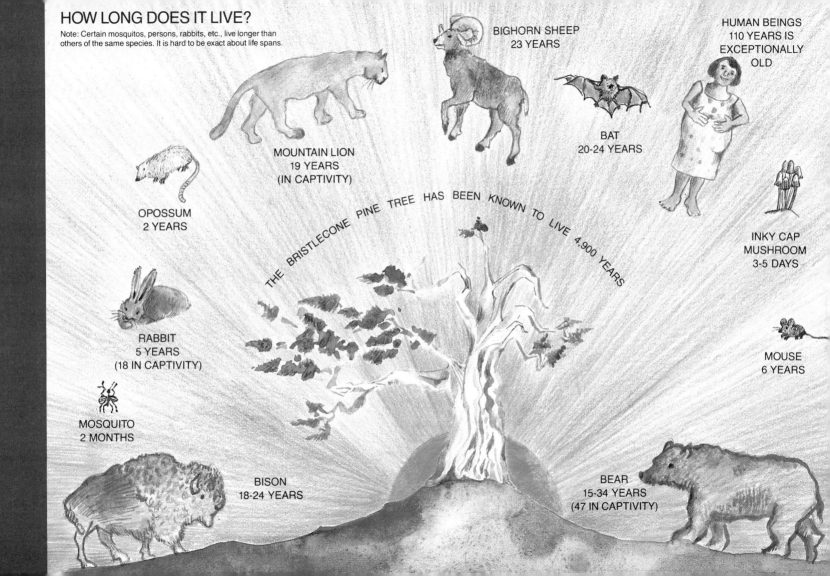

HOW LONG DOES IT LIVE?

Note: Certain mosquitos, persons, rabbits, etc., live longer than others of the same species. It is hard to be exact about life spans.

BIGHORN SHEEP
23 YEARS

HUMAN BEINGS
110 YEARS IS
EXCEPTIONALLY
OLD

BAT
20-24 YEARS

MOUNTAIN LION
19 YEARS
(IN CAPTIVITY)

OPOSSUM
2 YEARS

INKY CAP
MUSHROOM
3-5 DAYS

THE BRISTLECONE PINE TREE HAS BEEN KNOWN TO LIVE 4,900 YEARS

RABBIT
5 YEARS
(18 IN CAPTIVITY)

MOUSE
6 YEARS

MOSQUITO
2 MONTHS

BISON
18-24 YEARS

BEAR
15-34 YEARS
(47 IN CAPTIVITY)

POST CARD   POST CARD

HAPPY BIRTHDAY GRANDPA

Do you like this card? We went to see the
oldest living things in the whole world.
They are trees called Bristlecone Pine trees.
They are much older than you Grandpa.
One of them might need 4900 candles.
   The wind blows so much up here these
trees grow all twisted like corkscrews.
   It snowed here. It was hot when we start-
ed up. I didn't have my jacket. I froze.
But POTATO loved it. She chased snowflakes.

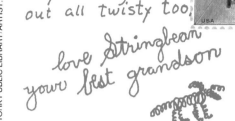

she should live
up here in summer.
Only she might come
out all twisty too.

love Stringbean
your best grandson

Mr. F. Muller

COE SPRINGS
MOTEL
JELOWAY, KS

66708

POST CARD

Hi Folks,
Stopped at this nice store to get a new lure I want to try. And new running shoes for Stringbean. His toes are growing right out his shoes. (They'll get to the Pacific before we do.)

And would you believe it?. the salesperson says to Stringbean, "you know just ½ hour ago there was a real circus clown sitting in that chair trying on our biggest shoes. But he only wanted to buy one." Stringbean's eyes bugged out! He ran and got the clown's shoe. He described the circus trucks to the woman. "That's them", she said.

I grabbed Stringbean (his face in a big chocolate ice cream cone) and we drove all over town looking. No luck. We've been calling them the Mystery Circus.

* Freddy bought
* me such great shoes
* and he let me take
as long as I wanted
to decide.
love S.

Coe Family
Coe Springs Motel
Jeloway, Ks.
66708

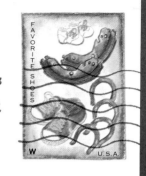

...love F

OUR SPECIALTIES

World's Best Coffee

Milkshakes

Blueberry Pie

Lemon Meringue Pie

Bacon and Eggs,
Just as You Like Them

Buttermilk Biscuits

Featherlight Pancakes

POST CARD

Dear Ma,

Don't you wish this place could be near Jeloway? We are worried about our money lasting. Fred says we shouldn't eat in any restaurants. But I never ate inside a <u>BOOT</u> before.

Tomorrow we cross the desert. Freddy says we need to start so early it won't even be light out. Freddy thinks of lots of important things. But he's too bossy. We made this pact for crossing the desert.

PACT

Fred promises not to tease and boss and Stringbean promises not to talk and talk all the time and not to <u>whine</u>

Cesar J. Coe

Fred Coe

P.S I do <u>not</u> talk all the time. I don't talk in my sleep but Fred snores ～～～.

FAVORITE PIG-OUT U.S.A

ELENA M. COE

THE BEST **COE SPRINGS MOTEL**

JELOWAY, KS.

66708

MANY FASCINATING SPECIES OF LIZARD CAN BE FOUND IN THE SOUTHWESTERN U.S.
HORNED LIZARDS OR HORNED TOADS, FOR INSTANCE, LOOK LIKE MINIATURE DINOSAURS.
THEY BURROW IN THE SAND AT NIGHT, CAN ALTER THEIR COLORING, AND WHEN
EXCITED SPURT BLOOD FROM THEIR EYES.

Dear Mapa and Grandpa,
    At last we saw the circus trucks
on the road up ahead of us. Fred
said it could be a mirage. But he was
kidding. (Anyway a mirage looks like water.)
    We were really catching up with them
this time. Then you know what happened?
One of our tires blew. ⭐ Harry went zigzag
all across the road till Freddy could stop
her.
    But guess who changed the tire? Your son
Cesar Stringbean J. Coe changed the tire.
Only Freddy had to help get the bolts off. And
it was so hot we had to get our potholders
to hold the tools. But meanwhile we lost the
circus again.
                        Stringbean

⭐ Remember we named the truck HARRY-THE-CHARIOT

ARTIST: JENNIFER WILLIAMS ▪ SERIES #1—ANIMALS ▪ NATURE CARDS

HAULING MELONS
IN THE 1920s

USA   USA
W

Coe Family
Coe Springs Motel
Jeloway Ks.
    66708

P.S. But we found a new pet.
It's just like the one on the
card.
PPS. It's Stringbean's pet not
mine.
How come you raised a kid who can't
let anything that crawls go by without
adopting it?
Potato hates this heat. She envies Lily
at home in the shade. How's Lily?
Love to all of you back there.
                                    J.

FUTURE PRESIDENTS USA

USPS MESSAGE CARD

Dear Post Office →TO MY ᵒʷⁿ MOTHER
please deliver   COE SPRINGS MOTEL
              JELOWAY, KS.
                 66708

DEAR MA,

    I MISS YOU. AND DADDY TOO.

    I MISS GRANDPA TOO. I MISS LILY TOO.

    THE OCEAN IS STILL FAR AWAY.

    FRED IS **VERY** MEAN.

    He made me let my lizard go.

                    love stringbean

P.S.   I have given up on finding that clown and giving back
his shoe.

TRAIN TRESTLE CAMPGROUND

A DRAMATIC SITE WHERE ROCKY MT. BIGHORN SHEEP SHOW THEMSELVES HIGH ABOVE THE TRESTLE. THIS TRAIN TRESTLE IS A FAMOUS EXAMPLE OF THE CONSTRUCTION FEATS OF RAILROAD AND BRIDGE CREWS WHO LAID THE TRAIN TRACKS ACROSS RIVERS AND SWAMPS, OVER MOUNTAINS AND DESERTS, FROM THE ATLANTIC TO THE PACIFIC OCEAN.

POST CARD

Dear Folks,

MADE IT ACROSS THE DESERT O.K!

Spending 2 whole days in this great campground. Washed all our stuff, washed Harry-the-Chariot, patched my jeans.

I'm worried about money. Might need to ask you to wire some.

Stringbean found some kids to play with. What a relief! Sending photos.

love, Fred

P.S. I don't hate Freddy anymore. He even lent his good fishing rod to my friends.

P.P.S. We didn't catch a <u>single</u> fish.

ARTIST: VERA B. WILLIAMS • GREAT CONSTRUCTION PROJECTS

P.P.P.S. But we found a snake. (Potato found it really.)

P.P.P.P.S. My friends are going to keep the snake.

P.P.P.P.P.S. We let that snake go.

COE FAMILY

COE SPRINGS MOTEL
JELOWAY, KS.
66708

JANIS AND JEANNIE'S
WORK WITH NATURE AND SHE'LL WORK WITH YOU is our motto.
Be sure to stop and try our produce.

Dear Folks,

They needed some extra pickers at a big strawberry farm down the road from this stand.

Stringbean saw the kids who pick with their families so he thought it would be fun. Ha Ha. Its a hard way to make not much money. They pay by the box and we were pitiful. Stringbean got so tired he even wanted to go home! He sure ate a lot of berries too.

By the way, you won't recognize little brother. Can't see his ribs anymore. He eats! You should have seen the size of those potatoes we baked last night, Grandpa!

ARTIST: JENNIFER WILLIAMS

P.S.
I never said I wanted to go home. Only Potato didn't like being tied up while we picked strawberries all day.

COE FAMILY
COE SPRINGS MOTEL
JELOWAY, KS.
66708

PUT YOUR BUSINESS ON A CARD

AND ANYWAY----→ NOW WE ARE ONLY 300 MILES FROM THE PACIFIC OCEAN

Tomorrow we drive straight there. I promised Fred, NO STOPS.

love, J.

W   U.S.A.
5 A.M.

Greetings from
the Pacific

THE PACIFIC OCEAN—
63,801,668 SQUARE MILES, THE LARGEST OF THE OCEANS.
LONG MAY IT CONTINUE AS HOME TO THE SEAL, THE WHALE, AND THE SALMON.

Dear Everybody,
    Stringbean Cesar Joseph Coe from the
Coe ~~Stringbean~~ Springs Motel in Jeloway,
Ks. is sitting on a rock with his feet in
the PACIFIC OCEAN
writing you this postcard.

    Ma, remember the ocean was in my
dream and you said maybe I would be
disappointed when I saw it for real.
Well I just want to tell you that I am not
even one little bit disappointed.

    And Potato just loves the beach. You
should see that dog chase waves.
                    Love Stringbean

PS We drove right through a giant redwood tree
on the way to this beach. Fire made a tunnel through it a long time ago.

ARTIST: JENNIFER WILLIAMS

FACTS ABOUT OUR PLANET CARDS

AMBER WAVES OF GRAIN

Dear Postman, Please take this
card 1500 miles to the

COE SPRINGS
MOTEL
JELOWAY, KS.
RIGHT IN
66708

I DID FIND THEM !

I really always knew I would. And they were right on the same beach with us. Only they were camped way down at the other end.

Potato and me saw their camp when we climbed up on the hill to watch for seals.

Now I am friends with the clown. He has a name that you can read backwards too. OTTO. He was so glad to get his shoe back. I can't exactly explain but he says each clown has very, very

special shoes just for that clown and no other clown has the same ones. S.

FAVORITE TOOLS

USA W

COE FAMILY

COE SPRINGS MOTEL

JELOWAY, KS. 66708

Dear Folks,
Stringbean is having the best time here. Potato is jealous of S's new friends.

see you soon   Fred

STRINGBEAN AND SOME FRIENDS
HE WENT FISHING WITH AT TRAIN
TRESTLE CAMPGROUND. [His friends'
mother took this photo especially
for Stringbean to send us.]

OTTO THE CLOWN
KINDLY SENT US THESE
PHOTOS.
STRINGBEAN SAYING HELLO
[AND GOODBYE] TO THE
SEALS FOR MR. MOE.
STRINGBEAN IN CLOWN
MAKE-UP AND OTTO'S TIE,
SOME CLOWN!!

CESAR WITH HIS CLOWN FRIEND

With thanks
to my friend
Cesar who found
my favorite shoe

Otto

Dear Ma, Pa, and Grandpa,

My name is not Stringbean anymore. Yesterday I changed it back to Cesar. I'm not even a little bit skinny now so I can't be Stringbean anymore.

I helped water the elephants this morning. I wish I could always live on the beach with the circus! But I would miss you and all my friends too.

THIS IS THE LAST POSTCARD I AM GOING TO SEND. I'M TIRED OF WRITING CARDS and Fred is going to drive back to Jeloway fast.

But wasn't I good? I did send one every day like I promised....Did you save them all like you promised?

your son and grandson

Cesar

USA

W

CLOWNS

COE FAMILY

COE SPRINGS MOTEL

JELOWAY, KANSAS

66708

POST OFFICE thanks for taking all these cards to my house.

PS There are still 4 oceans and lots of seas I haven't even ever seen!

ARTIST: VERA B. WILLIAMS ---- PLANETS, STARS, AND SPACE ----